Printed in the U.S.A.

ISBN 0-7172-8289-9

JIM HENSON'S MUPPETS
IN

# Kermit's Cleanup

## A Book About Imagination

By Michaela Muntean • Illustrated by Tom Brannon

GROLIER

Bean Bunny skipped up the front steps of Kermit's house and rang the doorbell.

"Hi," Bean said when Kermit answered the door. "Are you ready to go to the park?"

Before Kermit had time to answer, his mother called from the living room. "Kermit," she said, "don't forget about the basement."

"Oh, shucks," Kermit said with a sigh. "I did forget. Sorry, Bean, I can't go. I promised my mother I'd clean out the basement."

"It won't be as much fun without you," Bean said. "If I help you clean, maybe we'll still have time to go to the park. With two of us working, we'll be done hippety-hop."

"You mean lickety-split?" Kermit asked.

"Whatever," said Bean. "Come on. Let's get
to work."

So Kermit and Bean carried the cleaning
supplies down the basement stairs.

"Wow," said Bean as he looked at all the things in the basement. "This stuff looks great!"

"Are you kidding?" Kermit said. "It's going to be a lot of hard work sorting through everything. Then we have to lug things up the steps so my mom or dad can take them to the dump."

Bean pointed to a big box in the corner of the room. "You're not going to throw that out, are you?" he asked.

"Why would we want to keep it?" said Kermit. "It's not good for anything."

"I can imagine twenty things it would be good for, and that's before I really start using my imagination," said Bean.

Kermit looked at the box and then at Bean. "What kinds of things?" he asked.

"If we cut out windows and a door, it would make a great playhouse. Or we could turn it on its side and pretend it's a cave," Bean said.

"You're a good pretender, Bean," said Kermit.
"My granny bunny taught me all about
pretending. She calls it 'putting on your
imagination cap,'" Bean explained. "Granny
says there's lots of ways of looking at some-
thing. With an imagination cap on, you can
pretend all kinds of things!"

As Bean talked, he walked around the basement opening boxes and looking inside.

"Wow," he said, "you have some of the best
junk I've ever seen! Look at this box of old pots
and pans."

"What could we do with them?" Kermit

asked, looking puzzled.

Bean thought for a moment. "I've got it!" he said. "We'll turn that big box into a castle and we'll be knights."

"And the pots and pans can be our armor!" Kermit said.

"Now your imagination cap is starting to work," said Bean. "Come on. Let's get going!"

Kermit grabbed the broom and began to sweep while Bean hopped about with the mop, clearing dust and cobwebs from the ceiling.

When they had finished cleaning, they moved all the boxes and odds and ends to the middle of the basement floor. Then they set to work sorting out the things they could use.

While Kermit cut a door in the big box, Bean found two smaller, narrower boxes. He set them on top of the big box. "They are the towers on our castle," he explained.

In a corner of the basement, Bean found some old paint cans. One of the cans had some gray paint left in it.

"This will be perfect for painting our castle," he said.

Then Kermit found a small, blue wading pool. "This will make a great moat for our castle," he said.

Bean agreed. "Now your imagination cap is working full blast!" he said.

They used two cinder blocks and a plank to make a bridge over the moat.

Next, Kermit found a set of long, green
curtains. "Well, I guess we can throw these
out," he said.

"Oh, no," said Bean. "We'll hang them
behind our castle. They can be the forest where
the wicked dragon lives." So, with some old
garden hose, they hung up the green curtains.

Bean stepped back to admire their work.
"Now all we need is a horse," he said.

"How about using this old sawhorse?" Kermit
suggested.

"Great idea," said Bean.

First they painted the wood gray. Then
Bean placed an old boot on one end of the
sawhorse. Kermit wiped off the paintbrush
he had been using and tied it onto the other
end. When they were done, both Bean and
Kermit agreed they'd made a pretty good-
looking horse.

The basement was no longer a mess of boxes and stuff piled every which way. It now looked like a magical playroom.

"Everything is ready except for us," said Bean as he tied a pot lid on his head. He strapped a cookie sheet around his chest and picked up a spatula to use as a sword.

Kermit used a roasting-pan lid as a shield, a pot for his helmet, and a wooden spoon as his lance. He and Bean were two very fine-looking knights.

All afternoon, they rode their horse, fought dragons, and rescued princesses.

"This is the most fun I've ever had cleaning up," Kermit told Bean.

"My granny bunny was right," Bean
replied. "Everything can be more fun when
you're wearing an imagination cap!"

## Let's Talk About Imagination

Bean and Kermit had a big job to do. It might have been really boring. But they used their imaginations, and that made doing the job a lot of fun.

Here are some questions about imagination for you to think about:

What are some games that you play that use your imagination?

Are there some things that you have to do, like straightening up your toys, that you could make more fun by using your imagination? How could you do that?